P9-DWD-853

GIVE IT UP

STEPHANIE PERRY MOORE

THE *SWOOP* LIST #1

GIVE IT UP

STEPHANIE PERRY MOORE

MINNEAPOLIS

Darby Creek
A division of Lerner Publishing Group, Inc.
241 First Avenue North
Minneapolis, MN 55401 USA

For reading levels and more information, look up this title at
www.lernerbooks.com.

Cover: © Sam74100/Dreamstime.com (teen girl); © Andrew Marginean/
Dreamstime.com (brick hall background); © Andrew Scherbackov/
Shutterstock.com (notebook paper).

Interior: © Andrew Marginean/Dreamstime.com (brick hall background);
© Sam74100/Dreamstime.com, pp. 1, 43, 78; © Luba V Nel/Dreamstime
.com, pp. 10, 50, 85; © iStockphoto.com/kate_sept2004, pp. 18, 57, 93;
© Hemera Technologies/AbleStock.com/Thinkstock, pp. 25, 64, 100;
© Rauluminate/iStock/Thinkstock, pp. 33, 71, 108.

Main body text set in Janson Text LT Std 12/17.5.
Typeface provided by Adobe Systems.

Library of Congress Cataloging-in-Publication Data

Moore, Stephanie Perry.
    Give it up / by Stephanie Perry Moore.
        pages cm. — (The swoop list ; #1)
    Summary: Five diverse girls at a Jackson, Georgia, high school come
together to give each other support after learning that their names have
been placed on a mysterious list of girls with bad reputations, some for
legitimate reasons and others through no fault of their own.
    ISBN 978-1-4677-5804-8 (lib. bdg. : alk. paper)
    ISBN 978-1-4677-6049-2 (pbk.)
    ISBN 978-1-4677-6191-8 (EB pdf)
    [1. Conduct of life—Fiction. 2. Dating (Social customs)—Fiction.
3. Interpersonal relations—Fiction. 4. High schools—Fiction.
5. Schools—Fiction. 6. Sex—Fiction.] I. Title.
PZ7.M788125Giv 2015
[Fic]—dc23   2014014254

Manufactured in the United States of America
1 – SB – 12/31/14

For
Delta Sigma Theta Sorority, Inc.
Covington Area Alumnae Chapter
Cotillion Committee

Officers: Lisa McWilliams, Terri Belle, Melissa Mims. Co-chairs: Katrina Bilal, Sarah Lundy, Monique Jones. Subchairs: Serena Becton, Deborah Bradley, Michelle Bryant-Johnson, Joanee Buffaloe, Jenell Clark, Kathleen Henderson, Ijeoma Johnson, Celeste Jordon, Alethea Mack, Dionne Maddox, Clotiel Nelson, Leslie Perry, Shirley Perry, Jonnah Thomas, Lakeasher Thrasher, and Bridgette Williams.

We give up much to serve
our young people.
Thank you for helping me, as chair, help our
outstanding participants
waltz into greatness!

CHAPTER ONE

Labeled (Sanaa's Beginning)

On a gray and rainy day, Sanaa Mathis woke up just as gloomy. Now she was headed for school on autopilot. What had gotten her down was that her perfect Christmas break was over. She was with a guy who had her heart. They'd shared a special moment during the break, and the seventeen-year-old senior was in love. Miles Jackson reciprocated Sanaa's feelings, and he had even told her so. They went to the same high school in rural Jackson, Georgia, where not much went on. Most of the gals in school wanted Miles, including Sanaa's best friend, Toni Payne. In Toni's delusional world, she and Miles were an actual couple.

At the start of their senior year, Sanaa had every intention of being the good girlfriend to Toni and helping her work things out with Miles. Sanaa set out to talk to Miles on her shy friend's behalf, but something special developed between Sanaa and Miles instead. As hard as she tried to fight her growing feelings for the hot-chocolate hunk, nothing could be denied. The only thing she knew to do was hide the relationship from everyone, especially Toni.

"It's freezing," Sanaa said to her peers as they all entered Jackson High School.

No one responded. She just received tons of eerie looks from people. She didn't know if she had a stain on her clothes, if she stunk, or what, but it was odd. She didn't like the unsolicited attention. Sanaa got to her locker and stopped dead in her tracks. She saw a note posted on her locker. It was written on an obituary notice for a girl her age.

"Is this a joke?" Sanaa yelled out, but folks kept going.

Against her better judgment, she read the words:

Dear girl who's found her name on an unflattering list,

Being the most popular girl in school can be great—if it's for positive reasons. However, when the spotlight shines on you because of your scandalous ways, only a group of people in your same boat truly understand and care deeply enough to swoop in and keep you from sinking. Having been shattered by the list before, I'm just the one to guide you through, even if I do it from beyond the grave.

Don't be scared now. You've made your bed, so stop lying in it and get up. Pity party over. This stupid list isn't going to take another one of us out. I'm not there, but I'm with you, feeling your pain and seeing your shame. I'm swooping in to help you change the game. Redemption, faith, wholeness, boldness, and revenge—yes, revenge shall be yours. It may be dark for you right now, but the sun in your life will shine again. The swoop list is not your end. It will give you a new beginning.

Your angel, Leah

Sanaa's hands started shaking. She dropped the letter. All her insides were in knots.

Toni scared her, saying, "You might want to check this out!"

"You startled me," Sanaa said, grabbing the phone Toni was holding.

With cold eyes Toni boldly stated, "This was sent out to all the kids in the school. People are saying you're a slut."

"What is this?" Sanaa asked. Sanaa looked at the screen of Toni's phone. It showed a photo of a piece of white notebook paper with some writing on it. On the top of the page someone had written "The Swoop List."

"The swoop list?" Sanaa said looking at it.

"Yup, and read girl number one."

"Sanaa Mathis?"

"That's you, boo."

Sanaa stood there, shocked. "The swoop list, what is it?"

"It's a hot mess." Toni smirked.

Sanaa didn't know what was going on with her bestie. If the list was so bad, why was Toni acting happy she was on it?

Toni scrolled up her phone. "Here's the definition of the swoop list. One, a list of the top fast girls in a particular area. Two, a place where boys kiss and tell to humiliate girls they've been with. And three, names of shame to embarrass the so-called sluts of the school. Dang, Sanaa . . . who'd you piss off to get on this? I thought you were a virgin."

Sanaa couldn't look at her friend. She couldn't say, "the guy you wanted to get with has devoured me all apart." She could not admit she'd betrayed her friend, even though Miles had never liked Toni. Sanaa looked away.

"Oh, somebody's had a hotdog cooked in the oven," Toni joked. "Tell me, tell me, who is it?"

"Forget it. I have bigger problems than that right about now."

"Yep, this swoop list?"

People were pointing to their phones. They were calling her unflattering names. Sanaa felt like she was going to break.

Toni shouted to all the onlookers, "Go on about your business, guys! This ain't no peep show."

"Get out the way, Toni!" said this one thug named Ace who ruled the school. "I'm trying to get with the swoop list girl to see if she deserves being up there."

Toni didn't back down. "You move out the way before you don't have no balls left to try and get with somebody."

People were oohing and aahing. The talk about her was getting worse. Sanaa felt like she hadn't washed in days.

Sanaa tried to run away, but Toni grabbed her sweater. "I'm with you, sis. You didn't do anything to deserve being on this list. This has got to be a mistake."

Dropping her head, Sanaa said, "Well, who put me on it?"

Toni shrugged her shoulders. "I'm here for ya, though."

"Thanks for having my back with Ace. I want to go home. I knew when I woke up this morning this day was going south."

"Probably the guy you were with put you on the list. Trifling, huh?" Toni shook her head.

Sanaa wondered if it were possible.

***

Later that afternoon, Sanaa was at home in her room, lying across her bed and crying. She wanted to forget the whole day. She'd had food thrown at her, had been called all kinds of names, and had been propositioned by guys. No one would have expected Sanaa to face such humiliation. She was from a two-parent household where both parents worked hard to give her and her older brother—who was away at college—a good life. She had too much time on her hands, but she had never really gotten in trouble. How could she tell her parents she was being called a slut?

A text came through to her phone. She looked at it and saw it was Miles. "I'm at your front door. Come open up."

Huffing, she made her way to the front door. Immediately upon opening it, he grabbed her and started kissing her. His hands rubbed all over her body.

She stepped back. "Not today, Miles, no. I can't."

Showing his pearly whites, Miles pleaded,

"What? You worried about that pitiful little list? Please, I was getting props all day for that. Come on, babe."

He took her by the hand and led her down the hall towards to her bedroom. Truly feeling uncomfortable, she jerked away. He wasn't hearing her at all.

"What's going on? What's the problem?"

"Guys are giving you props, but they're calling me a slut. I'm supposed to be okay with that, and we just keep on going? Let's deal with how my name got on the list," she demanded.

Miles squinted. He started sucking his teeth. He was really checking out Sanaa's vibe.

Squinting his eyes, he said, "Babe, I know you don't think I had anything to do with it."

"Well, how else did my name get on there?"

"I don't know, and I don't care. I told you I loved you. You got me thinking about you all through school. I just want to be with you. Let me take your mind off all this."

He placed both of his hands in hers and gently pushed her towards the wall, lifted her hands in the air, and started kissing her passionately.

One thing led to another, and on the hall floor he had his way. She didn't ever remember saying yes, but Miles didn't care. When he was done, he didn't stick around to cuddle her or talk about how she was feeling.

"Peace, I'm out," he said.

Sanaa sat on the floor, half naked, and rocked back and forth. Suddenly, she felt like she deserved to be labeled.

CHAPTER TWO

Ostracized (Willow's Beginning)

Willow Dean was the envy of most girls on the dance team, and she knew it. Not only was she strikingly beautiful with her glowing, caramel-brown skin, fly-short 'do, and hot body, but she wasn't a shy girl. Far from it, Willow always spoke her mind. Most girls she hung around were intimidated by her presence. Most guys wanted to devour her, and she let them.

Willow rebelled a bit. Her mom was pastor of the most influential, yet controversial, church in the area. Either people loved being led by a female, or they thought it was heresy. Since Willow's mom focused more on her parishioners, and since her father was always on the road driving a truck, Willow raised herself and her brother, William, who was a freshman.

When the first day of school back from Christmas break was over, Willow headed to dance practice. It was basketball season, and at every game the dance team performed a different number. Willow choreographed most of the dances. If it wasn't Willow, it was bossy, uptight Hillary Jones. The two girls competed fiercely and never got along.

"You're five minutes late," Hillary said to Willow, rolling her eyes.

"But I'm here. Why you tripping?" Willow scoffed back, not backing down. She noticed the dance team girls whispering to each other. They were looking at her like they didn't want her around. "You guys need to get over whatever you're stressing about."

"We actually think you need to resign. The dance team has a rep to protect, and we just can't let trash bring all of us down," Hillary said as she stepped up to Willow.

Willow was no punk, and she had no problem getting in Hillary's face. Willow said, "Speak English, girl. What are you talking about? I make us look good."

"You make us look like we're strip-club dancers, not professional ones," Hillary argued.

Willow started to grin slyly. She knew what this was all about. They were haters. She got more attention from guys than all of them collectively. She knew it, and so did they.

"You know what? You're supposed to be teaching a dance today, Hillary. Show us what you got—or do I need to whip up something?"

"You need to leave," Hillary demanded as the other girls on the team gathered behind her. "We've got a code of conduct, Willow, and you sleeping around with a whole bunch of guys, bringing down the name of this dance troupe is not a part of it."

"Just show her!" uttered Tiffany, Hillary's skinny-tail shadow.

Hillary jammed her phone in Willow's face. "Here it is right here. All over the school. You're swoop list girl number two."

Swatting the phone away, Willow said, "I heard about this list. It's a bunch of hearsay."

"Supposedly they have pictures and stuff. It's a site where you can click on it and see some things you've been doing," Hillary boldly told her, daring Willow to click on the link for proof.

"Which one of y'all jealous heifers put my name on here?" Willow yelled.

"So you're not denying that there is probably video of you in compromising positions out somewhere? If there is, you're gone because it won't just be hearsay. But if you had any class about yourself, you'd drop out now. Nobody wants to be associated with this list. And none of us want to be associated with you."

Willow stood there, looking at Hillary like she wanted to punch her. She actually balled up her right hand. But seeing the other ten girls supporting Hillary, Willow went to the bleachers and grabbed her things.

"I'm not dropping out of this dance team, but I'm getting to the bottom of this. No one calls me a slut and gets away." Willow stormed away.

"If the name fits, slut," Hillary said and laughed.

Willow whirled around, took two steps, and punched her. The fight was on. Willow was winning.

A few minutes later, with mangled hair and a stank attitude, Willow sashayed her way out of the cafeteria where the dance team was practicing. Quite a bit of satisfaction was flowing through her veins because she realized she had whipped Hillary pretty bad. One of the ballers, fine, six-foot-three Isaiah Walden, bumped right into her on his way into the gym.

"Watch where you're going!" Willow shouted.

As he walked around her, she had a thought. She needed to know how she got on the list, so she turned right around and followed Isaiah into the gym. The coach wasn't there. It was just the players warming up. Out of the five starters, she had laid down with three of them before.

Following Isaiah like a little puppy—but with the bite of a pit bull—she barked, "Isaiah, did you put my name on some swoop list?"

"Girl, I got practice. You stupid."

Willow scratched her head. She was looking for Eric, the light-skinned point guard who had a little Puerto Rican in him. It had been a while since they'd been together, but he'd enjoyed what she had to offer. She needed to confront him too.

"Did you put my name on the swoop list?" she asked him.

"No," Eric said, trying not to laugh in her face.

Fuming, Willow turned. It had to be Sebastian's pretty-boy behind putting her name on this list. She was so mad because, out of all of them, she'd made his stock go up. In her mind, Sebastian owed her. *That's just like a chump*, she thought. *You help them out, they screw you over.*

Sebastian was tying his shoe on the bench. Willow sat down next to him and said, "Don't you have something to tell me?"

"No. We're about to have basketball practice. Don't you got dance stuff?"

"I might be off of the team because of some swoop list. Go on and admit it. You know something about it."

Kenny was a captain, and he was calling all the guys to come to the center of the court. Sebastian was grinning. Willow was fuming. When he tried to get up to head that way, Willow grabbed his practice jersey. "Nuh uh, we ain't finished talking," she said.

"Get your hands up off of me, Willow. You asked half the team. Clearly somebody who's got to ask three guys within five minutes if they put her name on a list deserves to be there. Face it, girl: you're a tramp."

The basketball players started giving him dap. For the first time ever, Willow felt like someone had stabbed her in her heart. Devastated, she jetted out of the gym.

As soon as Willow got home, she dived onto her bed. She sobbed uncontrollably like no other time in her life. It was one thing for her dance teammates to make her feel like she had the plague, but it was another thing for the guys she had been with to laugh at her expense. There was a knock on her door.

"Honey, you okay?" her mom asked in a caring voice as she came in and sat by Willow.

"I heard about some list. Swoop list?"

"It's nothing, Mom. Don't worry about it."

"Your brother told me what it stands for." Willow was silent. "Well, I know you're probably doing all kinds of things I wished you weren't, but the Lord . . ."

"Mom, just stop it. I'm not trying to hear a sermon."

Her mom stood up and said, "Alright, then I'll keep it real with you. No one deserves public shaming. People are cruel, so we pray for them. However, if the list is causing you to do some self-reflecting, then we'll reflect on the positive. I beg to differ. I know you are a young lady. I'm praying about all this negative. I don't like you being ostracized."

CHAPTER THREE
Worried (Olive's Beginning)

Voluptuous and sexy, Olive Bell was in the bedroom of her boyfriend's trailer, trembling, and it wasn't because it was cold in the place. Olive didn't have on a stitch of clothes, so she pulled the sheet around her, thinking she was waiting for Tiger, a local gang leader, to come into the room so they could have fun. Instead, there were two guys Tiger controlled looking to have their way with her.

"Don't be scared, little momma," Ice said as he sat on the bed.

"What you doing in here?" she said to the white boy with tattoos across his face.

Before she could get an answer, Shorty, a dude no more than five-four, came over to her. He was licking his lips. Suddenly, he snatched away the sheet.

"You guys better get out of here! Tiger will be here any second," Olive yelled, covering her body with her hands.

"We get to play with you today, Olive baby," Ice said.

Shorty unbuckled his belt and said, "Yeah, and don't act like you ain't gonna like it."

"Tiger!" Olive yelled out.

"What the heck?" Tiger said as he burst through the door, looking like he was mad at his boys.

Olive started smiling. She got out of bed, took back the sheet, and covered her whole body. She stood behind Tiger.

"They're coming on to me. I know these are your boys, but they trying to take what's yours. This ain't cool! Control your thugs!" Olive screamed.

"You don't think my boys would be in here trying to take you without my permission, do you? What kind of riffraff do you think I'm running?" Tiger shouted.

"You want me to be with them?" Olive questioned, thinking he surely didn't.

"If you love me, you will."

Olive started crying. Tiger motioned for his boys to leave the room. He came over to her and became gentler. He stroked her cheek and kissed her. "Do this for me."

"Why? You want me to be your ho?"

"It ain't like that, baby. I'm going to take care of you; just take care of me."

"I want to take care of you, not your boys."

"But you got me, though, right?"

Though she was devastated and torn because she loved him, Olive nodded. Tiger opened the door. Ice and Shorty came in. She slid her cover off. She laid on the bed like a brick. They were acting as if she was taking them on the ride of their lives. With each unwanted thrust, Olive knew something had to change.

***

All night Olive was unable to sleep. Usually the

noise in the group home kept her awake, but this time it was the demons replaying the events of the day that got under her skin. But she made it through. Olive had been on her own since she was six years old. One day her mom dropped her off at school and never came to pick her up. From then on, she bounced from foster home to foster home. Now she was in this group home with six other troubled kids, and most of them were boys.

When Olive got to school the next day, she searched for Tiger. She desperately wanted to let him know she didn't appreciate him putting her out there like that. Though she had gone along with it, now she was changing her tune. She had psyched herself up to tell him off, but as soon as she saw him, he raised his hand like he wanted to smack her. She clammed up.

He grabbed her by the arm and pulled her over to a corner and said, "We're through."

Devastated, she said, "What do you mean we're through? I did everything you asked me to do."

"And so it's over."

"What do you mean it's over?"

"What, you deaf? I don't want no girl who everybody thinks is easy."

"If people think I'm easy, it's because you put me out there like that!"

"I know, but that was supposed to be between us. Now look, the world knows," Tiger said as he shoved a crinkled-up piece of white notebook paper in her face.

It took her a second to read it: "The Swoop List." The first two names she didn't know, but the third one stood out, Olive Bell.

"Who did this? Who put my name on this list? What is this? Where'd you get this from? I, I didn't . . . you, you can't drop me because of this!" Olive finally got out the words.

"It's over."

Olive breathed deep to hold back the tears, but she lost control as water fell. The pain was unbearable.

Classes were about to start, but Olive was held up in a corner. She was so embarrassed. She had done the unthinkable for a boy she loved, but he didn't feel the same way at all.

"Charles, she's over here," Shawn, her blonde-headed, blue-eyed foster brother yelled out to her other foster brother Charles. Charles's skin was richer than chocolate.

"What is going on, Olive?" Charles stood beside her and asked. "We got weird vibes from Tiger and his crew."

"Yeah, and his boy Ice said we needed to check on you. What's going on?" Shawn asked.

Olive sobbed, "Nothing, just leave it alone, guys."

"Leave it alone? You expect us to go on like nothing is wrong?" Charles said.

"Yeah, if we need to whoop up on somebody, we can. We saw you come in late last night and use up all the hot water like you couldn't get clean enough. Somebody try to take something?" Shawn asked her.

"You were raped?" Charles shouted.

"Shhh!" Olive finally opened up and said, "No! No. And I don't need y'all's help, okay."

"Naw, forget this, man. Somebody messed with you. I'm sick of them feeling like they can pick on people and do any kind of thing. Tiger can't . . ." Charles said, completely upset and unable to finish.

Olive started to realize what she had already known for a while. These two weren't just foster brothers. They felt like real brothers. They had her back.

Olive tried to rationalize. "What you going to do? Go fight somebody? You get suspended again, and you're out of school! You think I want that on me? Come on, Charles, no! You got to calm your temper."

"She's right, man," Shawn said. "You gotta chill, Charles."

"So what? We going to let him take advantage of her? And we ain't going to do nothing? Come on. Let's go find these punks and deal with this crap. You down or what?" He looked at Shawn as he gave him the ultimatum.

Shawn saw Charles was serious. The two went to handle Tiger. Olive ran after them, clearly worried.

CHAPTER FOUR
Thrilled (Octavia's Beginning)

Octavia Streeter sashayed her self-tanned white skin into Jackson High School with a big, bold smile plastered across her face. It's like she knew something was about to go down. Whatever was brewing, she loved the idea of it.

Octavia had arrived at school late purposely. She'd always done everything right. Gotten great grades, not given teachers any problems, been a model student, but had it gotten her any-where? No. Absolutely nowhere. As a Caucasian student at a predominately African American school, she felt no one ever really paid her much attention. She didn't consider herself an ugly girl, but she didn't get all the guys—or any guys, for that matter—looking her way.

As she walked into the school building, George, a hottie she'd had her eye on for years, was smiling her way, and her eyes couldn't stop batting. She'd been trying to catch his brown eyes for months. She noticed people were checking out their phones, pulling out pieces of paper, and nodding as they whispered to others. She didn't even have to look to see what they were looking at. She knew. She was number four on the swoop list that had come out yesterday, and the thought thrilled her.

"So um, when we going to hang out?" George asked, running a hand through his brown hair.

"Anytime," Octavia said as she batted her eyes.

"How about after school?"

"Sure. That sounds great. You want to grab a bite to eat?"

"Naw, I want you to come over to my place," George said.

Octavia got a little lump in her throat. The

way George was looking at her was new. He sensed her hesitation.

"I need a ride home," he leaned in and said. "Is that alright? We can talk some, too, so I can get to know you better."

The way he was looking at her, she loved it, but at the same time it made her extremely nervous. She agreed to meet him after school. She agreed to take him home. But she wasn't agreeing to anything else, and she wasn't sure he understood that. Octavia decided she'd deal with all that later. For now, she was ecstatic knowing that she and George would be together.

***

Octavia was in her car, and she was jittery. She realized she hadn't thought this all the way through. She wanted George to like her, but her car, which was barely holding on, for sure wouldn't make a great first impression. The twelve-year-old hand-me-down was probably the last car in the parking lot that anyone in the school would want. But at least she wasn't walking. So she puffed up her chest, pulled up to the curb, and reached over to unlock the door so that George could get in.

"Hey, beautiful," he said, not commenting at all about the pitiful car. Instead, he stroked her naturally curly red hair.

"Where to?" she asked.

"Oh, we can't move just yet." George placed his hand on her thigh.

Chills went up and down Octavia's spine. She was feeling things she'd never felt before. Before she could breathe, he was kissing her so that all of the students in the school parking lot could see. She hadn't put the car in park, and because she was so excited, she accelerated and immediately stopped, throwing his body forward then back.

"I'm sorry, I'm sorry," she said, like he was going to get mad or something.

"That's alright, baby. I want to see if what they wrote about you is true."

She didn't know how to take that. She just wanted him to notice her. She just wanted to get to know him better. She didn't want him to think she was a prude. But he was taking the swoop list seriously.

Thirty minutes later, when they were inside the filthy, dirty apartment that he shared with his mom, he moved clothes out of the way and threw her on the couch, and then he was trying to get in her pants.

"No, no, no," Octavia uttered.

"What do you mean 'no'? You didn't think I brought you over here to talk, did you?"

"George, I like you," she said.

"And I want to give you something to like. You know what I'm saying?" He looked down between his legs.

Octavia found strength she didn't know she had and wrestled her way out from under him and stood up. "I'm a virgin."

George looked perplexed. "You're lying. You're on the list. Everybody knows you're easy. That's all everybody was talking about at school today. If you are pure, I ain't up for teaching nobody nothing. You need to go."

As she fixed her clothes, she watched George head towards the bathroom and slam the door. He yelled, "You know how to see yourself out. When I come out, you need to be gone. Leading people on. Crazy wench."

As the tears started to well up, Ocativa gathered her stuff and walked to the door, hoping he would come out and not be so cruel. She'd thought getting on the swoop list would get her close to the guy she'd admired for years, but now she wasn't feeling so good about making herself look so bad. What had she done?

***

It was Wednesday morning, and Octavia didn't have the same pep in her step as she did the day before. She knew she was on the swoop list and that people were talking about her. Somewhere deep within that didn't make her that upset, but it didn't give her the same pleasure as it had the day before either. She was beginning to see obscurity wasn't such a bad thing. Better to be unknown than known for something bad. But she knew the truth. She knew she wasn't what was written on the list. She could handle this.

Octavia spotted George. As she got closer she knew he was mocking her. She couldn't believe what she was seeing. George started giving the guys dab. He was making them think more happened than did.

"Was it good, man?" another guy asked.

George just looked like "What do you think?"

Octavia couldn't move.

"You don't need to go back for seconds, my turn now!" a girl with dreads said to George as she came over and rubbed his chest. "He can't talk to you," she said to Octavia. "You had your turn, boo. Everybody here knows George ain't a one-girl man."

"Yeah, I'm through with that," George boldly said, and he rolled his eyes at Octavia.

Octavia wanted to challenge him. But her mouth couldn't say what her brain was thinking. This joker had bragged that he'd been with her. Guys weren't looking at her like they were impressed anymore; they were looking at her like she was stank. People were laughing at her.

"Sticks, you can get with her!" George yelled back.

Sticks said, "Naw, dude, heifers on the swoop list nasty. Word's out they all got diseases and stuff."

Octavia wanted to run outside, get in her broken-down car, and go home. Being on the swoop list was the worst thing she could have wanted to happen. Now that she was standing alone and ostracized, she was not thrilled.

CHAPTER FIVE

Raped (Pia's Beginning)

Pia Alvarez sat in class, shaking. She couldn't believe the picture that her best friend Claire had just shown on her phone—it was a list with Pia's name as number five. She wasn't a hoochie, skank, or worse. No, Pia had been a good girl all her seventeen years of life. She was the shy Latina cheerleader on the mostly African American squad. All she wanted was to have a better life for herself than the one her single, struggling, working-sometimes and on-welfare-most-of-the-time mom's life afforded for the two of them.

Pia knew the importance of getting a good

American education. Her mom didn't have one, and as a result, her options in life were limited. Men came in and out of her apartment to spend time with her mom. Pia didn't judge, but she did vow that her life would be different. But now everything seemed messed up, and she couldn't take it.

"Ms. Alvarez, you're shaking," said Ms. McWilliams, her government teacher.

Pia didn't want to look up. She believed the shame she felt inside would spill out if she looked at her teacher. She turned away, but tears still dropped from both eyes.

"You know what, Pia? Come here." Ms. McWilliams, who was a no-nonsense teacher, stepped outside into the hallway with Pia. "I'm going to write you a pass. I want you to head on down there to see Ms. Davis."

Offended, Pia cried out, "I don't need to talk to a shrink."

"You need to talk to somebody."

She took the pass and reluctantly walked to the counselor's office. Ms. Davis was waiting. She invited Pia to sit on the couch. After ten silent minutes in Ms. Davis's calm and caring presence, Pia opened up. Her story came out in a rush.

"I'm on this list, and I don't deserve to be on it. The things that they are saying about me, that are going around the school, only happened one time. It's not because I willingly did it. But during the holidays, when we had that basketball tournament, we came back to the school, and I waited for my mom . . . guess she forgot all about me. So I was waiting around, and I could hear some guys laughing as they walked up behind me. I was grabbed, hit in the face, and thrown in a car. They took me to some dark road, and there three different guys forced themselves on me. I was dropped off at my apartment complex, so apparently they knew me. I was raped, and now my name is on some list like I asked for it to be there. Oh my goodness."

Ms. Davis didn't like seeing Pia rattled. "Just stay strong, Pia. We're going to get to the bottom of this."

"No, nobody can know." Pia stood up quickly.

"Okay calm down. Nobody will know. Okay? I won't push you."

"Am I going to be broken for the rest of my life?"

Ms. Davis hugged Pia until she calmed down. "No, dealing with this is going to make you strong. You won't be broken forever. I promise."

Pia didn't think Ms. Davis was telling the truth. Pia was having countless nightmares over the whole ordeal, and that scared her.

***

By day's end, Pia got herself together. School was finally over. The last place she wanted to go was cheerleading practice. Being one of the quiet girls, she always made sure she kept herself out of the drama. She loved cheering because she loved doing the wild, funky, buck cheers. But now everyone was talking about her. She was in the spotlight, and there was going to be no way around it. She didn't know how she was going to handle it when the girls started talking about her to her face. She wasn't a wimp, but she wasn't combative either. She wished she could just be alone in the locker room a little longer.

Claire, who was also a cheerleader, looked over and said, "Come on, we're going to be late. I'm not trying to run no laps."

"Did you ever spend time with that counselor lady?" Pia asked, partly because she was trying to stall and also because she really wanted to know. Ms. Davis seemed sweet. However, Pia was rethinking the session. She'd told her secret, and she wanted confirmation that the lady was trustworthy.

"Yeah, I told her one time when I missed a period."

"You did?"

"Yeah, you remember. Last year . . ."

"Yeah, but you weren't pregnant."

"I know. I went to see her before I knew I wasn't. She told me to relax, and when we calculated it all, she didn't think I was pregnant. When it turned out I wasn't, she had me come to this group with other girls who had pregnancy scares. She called herself our mentor. She made a lot of sense."

"What do you mean?"

"She just made me think about my future. She helped me see all the stuff that I'd have to give up if I had a baby. I just think she's all-around cool."

"I hope so. I shared something with her today."

Claire leaned in, expecting Pia to say something.

"Forget it, never mind."

"Y'all better hurry up and get on out here," Coach Reeves yelled, keeping Pia from revealing all.

Claire took Pia's hand and led her into the gym. As soon as Pia and Claire stepped out into the gym, their team captain Chancy and her groupies stared hard at Pia.

Pia found the strength within and said, "So what? Y'all want to talk about this thing or what? I don't know how my name got on the list."

Chancy said, "Obviously because you're too hot to trot, walking around here like you're the good senorita. Somebody been doing some salsa something."

"If you don't know that, then you need to shut your mouth," Claire said, getting Pia's back.

"One of the dance girls is on the list, and now people are talking about all of them." Chancy said. "We can't afford for our cheerleading squad to be trashed too."

"If you're on the cheerleading squad, it's already messed up," Claire said.

The two of them got in each other's faces. It wasn't until Coach Reeves blew the whistle that they came apart. Pia felt horrible.

A couple of weeks ago someone had taken her innocence. Now most of the girls she cheered with were trying to take away her dignity. She had to figure out a way not to let them.

***

Claire dropped Pia off at her apartment around four thirty in the afternoon. When Pia got into the apartment, she felt like she was going to throw up when she saw her mom and her mom's boyfriend sprawled out across the sofa in the living room, barely clothed.

"Mama!" Pia yelled, seeing too much of their disgusting, unfit bodies. "Can you two get up and go somewhere else?"

Her mom barely moved until, finally, after being jabbed enough by Pia, she looked up and said, "You're home already? I thought you just went to school."

Her mom was wasted. There were smashed beer cans, cigarette butts, and a bong on the coffee table.

Pia lost it. She screamed, "You're supposed to be taking care of me! I come home, and I have to take care of you! When are you going to be my mom? When are you going to care? When are you going to make something of your life?"

"Yeah, when are you going to do all that?" the man next to her mom called out, and then he giggled.

"Oh, Jim! Just get your stuff and go!" Pia's mom yelled.

Jim looked at Pia and licked his lips. "You let me do your kid I'll give—"

Her mom slapped Jim before he could

finish. Pia smiled wide. Jim couldn't believe he'd said something offensive.

"Get out of my house!" her mom yelled as she went over to the front door, opened it up, and pushed him out, not even caring that he was trying to put on his pants.

Pia went to clean up. She didn't want to take care of her mom, but that's all she knew to do. As she straightened, the tears kept falling. Her heart was breaking, not just thinking about how disappointed she was in her mother, but how much she hated her own life as well. Suddenly, Pia fell to her knees and really wept.

"I'm sorry, sweetie. Sorry I let you down. It's hard. I'ma do better. I promise."

"That's not it, Mom."

"Well, what's wrong? Talk to me."

"You don't care about me."

"If I didn't care about you, I wouldn't be giving my body to feed your butt," her mom answered with slight anger in her voice.

"It's not like I asked you to do that. If you knew what was going on with me, you'd make sure I'm alright." "What you going on about?

What's wrong with you?"

Tired of not being real with her mom, she said, "Mama! A couple weeks ago I was raped!"

CHAPTER SIX
Pissed (Sanaa's Middle)

Sanaa was fed up with folks at Jackson High School talking about her. She was also tired of Toni, her so-called best friend, pretending to her face that they were cool. Yet Sanaa saw Toni's true thoughts and feelings shining through in things she was posting about Sanaa online. So when Sanaa saw Toni huddled with some other girls at school, she just kept walking.

Toni said, "Hold up, Sanaa! What's wrong with you? Walking past people with your nose all in the air and stuff."

"What were you doing over there talking to them? You know they don't like me. Then you expect me to go over and act like we're all good."

"So what are you trying to say? If I'm friends with them, I can't be friends with you?"

"I'm not saying anything. I kept walking. You're the one following me."

"Okay, what's up your butt? Or should I say who? Because I've just been trying to figure this whole swoop list thing out. Whatever guy you were with, he obviously sold you out. But you saying it wasn't anybody so . . . you know how people start rumors."

The way Toni said that, Sanaa knew there was more to what was being said than met the eye. She felt that deep down, Toni was happy her reputation was soiled. That hurt her.

"Where you going?" Toni asked when Sanaa turned back around to head towards the ladies room.

"Going to the bathroom! Is that a problem?"

"No, let's go to the other one down the hall, like in the direction we were walking."

"What do you mean go to another one? It's right here. I'm going to go in here and use the bathroom. I'll catch up with you later."

"No!" Toni stood in the doorway, trying to block Sanaa from getting through.

But Sanaa moved her girlfriend out of the way, and she was frozen in her tracks when she saw the girls Toni was just talking to with permanent markers. They'd already written "Sanaa" on a stall door, and she didn't want to think what was coming next. Sanaa was speechless.

One of the girls, Gina, smirked. "Don't be mad. We're just putting the truth in writing. If you're a trick, you're a trick."

Sanaa rushed over, knocked the pen out of Gina's hand, and gave her a hard punch.

***

Sanaa was in the principal's office before she calmed down. And a few minutes later she'd shuffled down to the counselor to discuss her "issues." Her arms were folded, her eyes were red, and her legs were crossed. She completely looked like she did not want to talk, much less open up about her personal problems.

Ms. Davis had a warm smile on her face, but she finally got real and said, "You're not going anywhere until we have a frank discussion about what's going on. I've seen the unfortunate swoop list. I'm fully aware your name was at the top of the list. You've had a rough week, and that has got to have you feeling some type of way."

Sanaa realized Ms. Davis was not going to quit until she talked.

"Yeah, and it's crazy because I got this letter that's apparently from a former swoop girl who says she's dead, but wants to help me."

"Really," Ms. Davis responded, leaning in to hear more.

"Yes, it is eerie to think of a dead girl wanting to look out for me so I don't end up like her. But this whole list isn't fair. I've only been with one guy. And that he'd betray me like this and put my name on the list is hard to believe."

"So you think he told?"

"I don't know. I thought he loved me. That's why we took it to a whole other level. But I should have known he was like all the other jerks."

"Have you broken up with him?"

"No, because I guess deep down I don't think he sold me out. They're painting me to be some freak. I used to think about sex all the time, but that wasn't my fault. And if he would have just not shown me those pictures when I was little," Sanaa said with anger in her voice, like she wanted to take the face of her abuser, put it on a dartboard, and throw darts at it.

Ms. Davis sat down next to Sanaa. "You can talk to me. What's spoken in here stays in here. It sounds like you've got some past hurt."

With her head down and feeling ashamed, Sanaa uttered, "Yeah, my parents and I would be over at my cousin's house. They'd be upstairs playing spades, and my cousin and I would be downstairs. When I was in the second, third, and fourth grades, I would go over his house, and my cousin who was in college would show me all this porn. I just started thinking about sex too soon. So when I finally got a boyfriend who wanted me, I wanted him. If I'm a freak, if I'm a slut, if I'm a swoop list girl . . . it's not my fault."

Though Sanaa had tears dropping from her face, she was angry and completely upset about her past. Something about letting out the past hurt and talking to Ms. Davis was helping her heal. Releasing the tough emotion felt good.

***

Sanaa gave Ms. Davis a big hug. Then she stepped out of the counseling office and back into the crazy world of high school. Just as she rounded the corner, two guys from a known gang got in her way.

"Swoop list girl number one," Ice said to her. "Oh, that booty is tight."

She'd just gotten out of the office, dodged the bullet of getting in trouble for fighting a girl, and now she was ready to take on two guys who felt like she owed them something. Not today. If she got suspended, so be it. She wasn't going to be touched by chumps.

"Get your hands off of me!"

"Naw, I want my hands all over you!" Ice said.

Sanaa knew those guys didn't care about school. They had nothing to lose. Even if they took her right there in school, they wouldn't care, but she cared. Ice barely had a grip on her, and he was laughing at his own lame joke, so she kneed him in the crotch. He fell to his knees, and she took off. She ran—straight into Miles, and he was looking at her like he had seen the whole thing. But he hadn't done anything.

"Why didn't you help me?" she asked.

When he shrugged, she tugged away from him. Miles had showed he was a punk. Sanaa ran away, pissed.

CHAPTER SEVEN
Vented (Willow's Middle)

Willow's life had turned upside down, and she needed help turning it right side up. The last couple of days she'd thought heavily about who could have put her name on the swoop list. But honestly, she'd probably been with more than ten guys in less than ten months, and that was being modest. She remembered that when she was a freshman and started her period unexpectedly, the guidance counselor Ms. Davis helped her out immensely. Though she hadn't been back to the divulge intimate details of her life, she knew it was high time for a counseling session, so she got her physics teacher, Miss Sherman, to write her a pass to do just that. As Willow rounded the corner, she bumped hard into someone.

"You need to watch it!" Willow screamed.

"I'm so sorry," a girl threw her hands up and said.

"Wait, you're Sanaa Mathis, right?" Willow asked.

"Yeah, and . . . so what?" Sanaa replied, still upset from bumping into the gang guys.

"We don't hang, but now we've got something in common. I don't know if you know me, but I'm Willow Dean. I'm number two on the stupid swoop list. Actually headed to the counselor because my week has been a disaster. Are you okay?" Willow asked, seeing that Sanaa looked shaken.

"It's just a lot. I certainly get it being a disastrous week, that's for sure. But I just left Ms. Davis. You should talk to her. She was cool."

"Yeah, thanks. We've got to keep our heads up," Willow said, wanting Sanaa to toughen up. "When people try to pull you down, you best believe you conquer them by keeping your head up and not letting them get to you."

Sanaa smiled. Each went her own way. Willow knew most of the girls in the school with a fast reputation before the swoop list ever came out, and Sanaa wasn't in that crowd.

Before Willow could get too far away, Sanaa yelled out, "Willow!" Willow turned around.

"Don't go that way. Some thugs are over there."

"Who?"

"Some fools in the gang Black Oil."

"Ice?" Willow asked.

"Yep."

"Alright, thanks. You're right. Trouble follows them. I will go the long way. I appreciate that, Sanaa."

"No problem. You said we've got to look out for each other."

"Yeah."

They exchanged numbers. Willow walked on and thought maybe she needed new friends. Sanaa might be the right type.

*****

"Ms. Davis, you got a second?" Willow said as

she tapped on the door.

"Yeah, come on in. I've been thinking about you."

"What? Since you've seen my name plastered all on some dumb list? Idiots. I wish whoever put my name out there would have come to my face and said whatever they had to say."

"Alright, calm down. Willow, where did all this start for you?"

"At choir rehearsal. I had to be at church all the time. And when our parents were in Bible study, we'd be playing hide-and-seek. And some of the places we hid were mighty tight quarters—bodies touching up against each other—and people just started exploring. My body started developing at the same time. The older guys started liking me, and they started showing me more stuff. The more I learned, the more I wanted it. When I'm with a guy, it just goes far real quick. I don't see him standing in front of me with all his clothes. It's like I imagine him with no clothes on, and I wonder if he's better than this one or that one. I don't know. I just left science class. I guess it's like a science experiment for me. I was fine in my own space. I wasn't trying to pass myself off as a virgin or anything like that, but I ain't need the whole world to know my business. It's like folks are looking at me like I'm dirty or something."

"You're not dirty. And you don't deserve to be on this crazy list. No one does. But you also have to know you're living a dangerous lifestyle . . . possible pregnancy risks, venereal diseases, and emotional scars. You are worth way more than what you're giving yourself credit for."

"I used to just have to have it. But, I mean, now that all this has come out . . ."

Willow couldn't finish her thoughts. She just dropped her head, utterly embarrassed. Ms. Davis placed a hand on her shoulder, then lifted her chin up.

"It's your body, so you have to decide what is right for you. Still, you need to remember to be safe with everything you're doing. And, you need to respect yourself enough to choose to be with guys who respect you, too."

Willow nodded her head in understanding.

She sighed. Inwardly, she couldn't deny the swoop list had awakened her. Maybe jumping from guy to guy was causing her to miss out on having a real, meaningful relationship?

***

When Willow got home, both of her parents were sitting on the couch with their arms crossed. Her dad was usually on the road with his truck, but today he was home. Her mom was usually headed to church to tend to her flock, but she was home waiting on Willow too. Willow knew she was in trouble.

"Wassup now?" Willow said.

"We went on your Facebook page today," her father said.

"What do you mean you went on my page?"

Her mother said, "Girl, you better get some sense, trying to talk all smart like you own something. We bought the computer, we can go on it."

"But my password . . ."

"It's not that hard to figure out," her younger brother, William, said from around the corner.

"Oh, I'm going to get you. Urgh!" Willow promised.

"Calm down, girl, you had to give us those passwords," her mother reminded her.

"But that's not even the issue," her dad began. "What're all these boys talking on social media stuff about how they've been with you? Me and your momma live our lives in such a way that we are a good example. We did not raise you to be fast and . . ."

"Okay, Dad, okay! Please quit acting like you and Mom are perfect. I've seen you watching X-rated movies when Mom is sleep. Mom, I've seen your diary and read where you talked about your toy you can't live without," Willow said, holding nothing back. She wasn't going to be crucified by her parents, who weren't as pure and innocent as they wanted her to believe. Their bubbles were burst.

"I admit I've got some stuff to think about, but cut the hypocrisy," Willow vented.

CHAPTER EIGHT
Crazed (Olive's Middle)

Finally it was Friday, and Olive was ecstatic about that. She'd had such a hard week. Her foster brothers had been protecting her. She hadn't had any run-ins with Tiger. She still was beating up on herself for thinking that she loved Tiger and actually thinking that he loved her. He didn't. Problem now was word was out that he wanted to destroy what she called her family.

"Okay you two, promise me there's not going to be any fighting. He's not even worth it," Olive said to Charles and Shawn as they got off the bus.

"Please, he's calling us punks all around the school," Charles said. "I'm not having it, Olive. I'm just not. It is one thing to break up with my foster sis, but to tell the world you let your boys run a train on her and . . ."

Not able to hear any more, Olive turned away. Though it was the truth, she didn't want to listen. Charles sensed her embarrassment, and he stroked her back as they went into school.

Tiger and his Black Oil boys walked into school and strolled right up to her two foster brothers. Since Charles looked like he was not backing away, the two of them eyed each other down. A crowd formed.

Charles said, "Negro, you must not know who you're messing with. I don't play, telling people you're going to get me."

"Whatever, I'll see you after school. You taking up for her like you want to get with her," Tiger said as he popped Charles in the chest.

Charles grabbed Tiger's collar. He was about to hit him. Olive's other foster brother stepped between them.

Shawn said, "Come on, man. Let's go."

Charles yelled, "Naw, move. He gonna try me. I need to beat him for what he did to Olive."

Tiger laughed.

Charles was trying to get loose so that he could get a jab in. Shawn wouldn't let him go. Olive was pacing back and forth.

"Prepare to die," Tiger said as he was being pushed down the hall.

"See, I'ma die or go to jail," Charles said to Olive as she held on to his shirt.

Tears were all in her face. "I know you care about me, but you can't do this with him. He is so not worth it. Don't let him make you lose it."

Charles jerked away from her and walked in the opposite direction. Olive was terrified. She knew their threats were not idle.

***

Olive and Charles had PE the same period. She was in an all-girl class, and they played volleyball. Charles's class full of boys played flag football, and they came inside dirty. She sat on the bleachers outside the boys' locker room, waiting on him to exit so that she could talk sense into him. But it was taking forever, or so she thought. She kept tapping on her knee and sighing as if he could see her impatience and speed up.

When the boys' PE coach came out, he said, "You need to go on to lunch. I don't know who you are waiting on, but nobody is in there."

"I just need to sit here for a second, Coach," Olive said, stalling since Charles hadn't come out.

"Well, do I need to write you a pass to the nurse or something?"

"No, sir. I just need to sit. I'll be okay."

"Well, I'm not going to leave you in here. But I do need to go pick up those cones from outside. If you're not feeling better when I return, I'll take you to the nurse myself."

"Yes sir, Coach."

Everyone knew Coach Court didn't play games. He was tough, not just on his very successful football team, but on every student in the school. He made the boys pull up their pants. He also had a rep for sending girls to the office if their clothes were too revealing.

As soon as the coast was clear, she went into the boys' locker room.

"Charles!" she yelled out, stunned to see Charles's wet body standing there with a towel half draped around his waist.

"What you doing in here?" he said, not covering himself.

"I . . . I was trying to talk to you," Olive said, trying to compose herself.

"So you couldn't wait until I came out?"

"Sorry," Olive said and turned to leave, upset.

But he put his arms out and stopped her. They looked each other eye to eye. In that moment, something was happening between them. Instead of addressing it, she dashed out of the boys' locker room.

***

About ten minutes later, Olive was in the lunchroom, trying to eat, but she kept visualizing the sight of Charles's muscular, wet body, and her heart couldn't stop pounding. Shawn had always joked that there was a connection between them, but both of them denied it. But now she knew there was no way she could deny the fact that something was going on, and it bothered her, so she couldn't face him. She'd waited all that time to walk with him to the cafeteria to convince him not to fight, and when she found him, she'd dashed away as fast as she could. Sitting alone and biting into her pizza, she was startled when Charles sat down beside her.

He said, "What was all that about back there?"

"What was what?" she said, unable to look at him.

"You know. You felt something."

They weren't touching, but she felt his warmth. Then feelings she never felt for her ex-boyfriend started to flare up. She needed to use her influence to convince Charles to chill, but she knew she didn't have much time when she saw Tiger and his boys darting towards them across the lunchroom.

"Listen, you can't fight Tiger," she said.

Charles wasn't listening to her. Seeing Tiger heading over, Charles pushed back from the table abruptly. As soon as Tiger came over, he tried to give Charles a right hook, but Charles had his hand out and stopped the balled fist with one cool motion. The crowd that was gathering started cheering for Charles. Tiger didn't like it, not one bit. He came back and charged at Charles, and they landed on the crowd. The two started tussling before Olive could scream "Stop!" Charles got in a couple of punches, but when he stood up to walk away, Tiger stood up and pulled out a gun. Everyone in the crowd ducked. Charles stretched his arms open wide.

"What? You that big and bad you want to do something?" Charles yelled.

"Don't be stupid, Charles!" Olive screamed out.

Charles said, "Just go, Olive. You can't rationalize with a fool who's crazed."

CHAPTER NINE
Realized (Octavia's Middle)

Octavia couldn't believe her eyes. Before her were two guys wrestling. And a gun. Where was the gun? At first everybody was cool standing around, but mayhem ensued as folks realized this was serious. Octavia saw Shawn as she jetted away and clutched his collar to tug him away too.

"Octavia, go," Shawn said.

"You're my boy! You gotta come too."

"Out the way, Octavia. I'm not going to sit here and let Charles go down."

"Please come, the gun could go off. We've known each other since what? Middle school?

I'm not leaving you." Octavia hugged him, seeing the rage in his eyes.

Feeling the closeness, she knew there was no way she could let him go. However, Shawn was determined to get Charles. Every time Shawn headed toward Charles, Octavia grabbed him.

Charles and Tiger were fighting hard. People were running to and fro. And then the gun went off.

It was like Octavia's heart stopped beating. Seeing the panic on Shawn's face broke her heart because they both knew Charles could be gone.

"Go on and get yourself out of here!" Shawn said to her.

"I'm not leaving you," Octavia replied, though fright consumed her.

Then the school resource officers flew around the corner with some administrators, trying to get everyone to get to class. They were radioing the police. Charles was moving. Relief passed over both Octavia and Shawn.

"I've got to help him get away," Shawn said as Octavia turned for them to leave. "He could get expelled."

Another girl ran over to Shawn. She looked familiar, but Octavia couldn't place her. As they hugged, Octavia realized it was Olive, the girl who lived at the foster home with them.

"We've got to help Charles," Olive said, but her eyes told Octavia she wanted Octavia to stay out of their family's business.

Though Octavia didn't want to, she stepped back and watched the two of them quickly grab Charles, who, thankfully, was okay. He hadn't been shot. They all ran. Shawn looked back at her. She smiled at him. But as she saw Tiger pick up his piece and flee, she realized it still wasn't over.

***

Octavia stood by the door of the counselor's office while all the teachers and administrators were trying to get students to get back to class. So much had gotten out of control, and all she had wanted was a little attention. She thought being on the swoop list would make her popular, but the last few days, the brutality she'd endured proved that being associated with the list was the worst idea she ever had. Now she wanted to talk about it. The principal, Mr. Way, came by.

"Young lady, you need to get on to class," he said, and he went on with his work, writing people up and sending others to his office.

"I'm here to see Ms. Davis. I—"

Mr. Way cut her off. "Not today. We've had a school shooting. We're on lockdown."

Ms. Davis walked up. "What's going on, Mr. Way?"

He huffed and said, "This young lady needs you."

With a calm voice, Ms. Davis assured him, "Oh, that's fine. No worries."

"Alright, keep her with you. It's just always something," he voiced in frustration.

Ms. Davis said, "Come on in. It's getting a little scary around here, huh, Octavia?"

"Yes, ma'am."

"So, you're on the swoop list. You're one of the quietest girls around here. How did that happen?" she asked.

Octavia looked up at the ceiling, looked

down at the floor, and made crazy faces with her mouth, all in an effort to divert the question. She wanted to talk. However, she was nervous.

"Can I be honest?" Octavia asked and was happy to see Ms. Davis nod. "I'm tired of always being the sweet girl; niceness gets you nowhere."

"But is negative attention the kind you want?"

"No," Octavia admitted. "But I haven't enjoyed being the last one guys ever look at. I get that I'm a minority in this school, but I want action. I guess I just didn't totally think the swoop list through. I wasn't trying to go from a sweetie pie to a hottie tottie."

"How'd your name get on the list?"

"Do we have to talk about all that? I just wanted to come to you because I realized, however my name got on the list, I was wrong for pushing it. But can I fix it?"

"Honey, that's a question only you can answer," Ms. Davis said, leaving Octavia truly confused.

***

After the last bell rang, Jackson High was still chaotic. Camera crews were there, and tons of parents and police were all in search of the gunman. They were interviewing students, but no one was talking. Everyone knew to be quiet, or else. When they were finally dismissed, Octavia was heading to the parking lot when Ice came up to her and pinned her on the hood of her car.

"What are you doing? Get off of me!"

Ice slapped her. "I saw you talking to the principal and talking to the counselor today. And you were over there with Shawn. You gonna try to turn us in or something?" Octavia was shaking. "And you've been holding out on everybody, quiet little girl on the swoop list. Somebody been hitting it. They ain't going to be the only one."

Ice reached down between her legs, spread them apart, and inched his way closer. Though they were both fully clothed, she felt sick.

"Please! Get off of me. I wasn't saying anything," Octavia shrieked.

"Dude, step off!" Shawn yelled, rushing over.

Octavia couldn't see where he was coming from, but she knew he was there. As she closed her eyes, she felt the weight of Ice's body lift away. All she wanted to do was go, but the two guys were fighting.

"You want to mess with somebody? You tryna rough up my friend?" Shawn demanded.

"Oh, that's why y'all were all together. This who put you on the list? The two of y'all got a little something going on. Well, if she fast, she fast," Ice said.

Ice shouted many more insults. Shawn lost it and hit him over and over and over like he was a punching bag. Octavia touched the back of his shoulders.

She screamed, "Please stop! I'll take you home!"

Shawn finally stopped. He got in her car, and she drove away. She looked over at his bloody hands, and tears dropped.

He just touched her chin with his unharmed hand, stroked her brow, looked her in the eyes, and said, "I couldn't let him hurt you. That's what I realized."

CHAPTER TEN

Intensified (Pia's Middle)

Finally, the long week was over. Pia was trying to get ready to go back to the school to cheer. It was Friday night, and though there had been a gunshot scare at the school and the principal wanted to cancel the basketball game, students and parents thought life should go on as normal. So Jackson High School was hosting boys' basketball.

Instead of her mom taking her straight to the gym, they made a stop before they got to the school.

"Mom, where ya going? I got to be back at the school at five."

"The place we're going closes at five, so you'll be there a few minutes late. If I need to talk to the coach, I will. You're seeing a doctor."

Pia and her mom hadn't fully talked. She knew telling her mom that she'd been raped was a lot. She didn't mean to make her mother feel bad, but she and her mom both knew Pia didn't have a great example. Even though her mom didn't always take care of business—like having regular meals at home—she loved Pia, and she wanted her to have a better life. Pia's mother got pregnant young, but she'd never told Pia the reason that her dad wasn't around was because she was raped as well.

"What are we doing at a gynecologist office, Mom?" Pia asked when they pulled up to the red brick and mortar building. Pia was scared.

"We're going in here to get you checked. You could be pregnant. I already made you an appointment," her mom said in a shaky voice.

"Huh? Mom, there is no evidence. It's been weeks."

"I know, but our cycles are the same time, and you haven't had one. You haven't wanted to eat, either. Something is going on."

Because of the whole swoop list thing, Pia had forgotten about her period this whole week, but it was overdue. She'd been sick on her stomach, but she thought that was just because her world was upside down. She was getting a little pudgy, too, and her breasts were tender. Was her mom right?

Forty-five minutes later, after they saw a doctor, it was confirmed.

***

"Pia, you don't need to be going to any basketball game. You need to rest up for tomorrow," her mother said to her as they drove to the school.

Pia heard her mom's words, but they were definitely going in one ear and out the other. She had to go to the game. She didn't want to go home, sit there, and think about a life growing inside of her that her mom wanted her to destroy. How could she keep the little life, knowing it was the result of her being blindfolded, forced down, and taken advantage of by three different males? Cheering, even though she had to deal with the drama of her fellow squad members, was the only thing that gave her joy. She desperately needed happiness to bring her out of her pit of gloom.

"If you just insist on going to this game, that's fine. But I'm not going to be able to bring you home. I have to take this car back over there to Jim."

"This is Jim's car? I thought you were through with him! I'll get a ride home, Mom," Pia said, truly frustrated and wishing that her mom would hug her and tell her that it was okay. Truth be told, how could everything be fine? Pia was also stressing because she had to wait for the results of an HIV test.

When she got to the game, she stood alone. Her girlfriend Claire stretched with her and asked what was wrong. Pia didn't say.

When they went over a few cheers, one of the girls shouted, "Pia, you're giving half effort. Put more into it."

So to shut her up, next time they practiced the cheer, that's exactly what Pia did, except she made herself sick and ran straight into the girls' bathroom. She knew what was wrong. It had already been confirmed. No way she was going to let the squad know. When she came out, she was more chipper.

"Sorry, you guys. The flu."

"Yeah right the flu," Chancy sneered. "You can hardly fit your uniform."

Claire said, "Forget her . . . you're fine."

Chancy teased, "And you can't keep stuff down either. You ain't got a bun in the oven, do you, swoop girl?"

Pia rolled her eyes and ran back towards the restroom. She ran right into one of the basketball players, Stephen Garcia—sheer perfection in her eyes. He was six-three, had muscles bulging, and had a gorgeous, honey-tanned Hispanic face. He was known to be a sweetie pie with a taste for chocolate sisters.

"Hey, I'm sorry," Stephen said to Pia. "You okay?"

Pia was uncomfortable being touched. She

dashed away, then looked back. Something about Stephen seemed familiar. It wasn't his touch or his breath, it was his smell. Unable to make it to the bathroom, thinking about where she knew the smell from, she rushed to the nearest trash can and vomited.

***

Pia wanted to scream. She lay on the sterile table with her legs up in the stirrups as the doctor performed the procedure ending her pregnancy. She so wanted it all to be a nightmare and not her reality.

"I know this is a little uncomfortable, but you're going to be alright," the doctor said.

She wanted to wring his neck. How dare he say she was going to be alright? The only thing that gave her solace was the fact that she hadn't asked for any of this. Those boys forced themselves on her. How could she love a child when she hated how it was conceived?

Finally, when the procedure was over, she rested for a minute and just cried and silently prayed, *Lord, I'm sorry. I could say my mom made me do this, but I know I'm not ready to be a mom. I know that's no excuse. I know you could have helped me make a way. I know teen pregnancy isn't the end, but Lord, I would have no help. I don't even know who did this to me. I want you to make them pay for the rest of their lives, but how can I say that when I ended a life before it began?*

Pia punched the table. She wished she could punch herself, but she kept thinking about Stephen. There was something about the way he said he was sorry. Did he hold the key? Did it even matter now? Of course it mattered, because, although there was no baby, Pia's anger intensified.

CHAPTER ELEVEN

Rattled (Sanaa's Ending)

Sanaa had endured the worst week of school she'd ever had. Life was supposed to be great. She was a senior. She had a man. She had a best friend. She had self-esteem. But all of the last three were sketchy at best, so going to school, even though it was a new week, was the last thing she wanted to do.

She pulled into the parking lot late. She actually drove around before going to school and contemplated going home. But she stayed.

Sanaa got out of her car and saw a girl stooped down by the passenger side of another car, bawling. "You okay?"

The girl didn't lift up her head, instead she pointed. Sanaa struggled to see what she was alluding to. When she saw the letters *H-O* on the trunk of the girl's car, she knew the girl was not alright.

"Don't even worry about this. Don't let it get to you," Sanaa said, not even knowing who the girl was, but understanding how bad it felt to be called such a horrible name.

When she lifted the girl up, she was surprised to see it was Willow. She didn't know Willow much, but she remembered exchanging numbers with her in the hallway days before. Sanaa had really felt a connection.

"It's me. Sanaa. We can't let anybody get to you. It's a new week for us both."

Willow screamed back, "I am what this says I am, okay? I thought I was okay with it. What's wrong with girls wanting to have a little fun? Guys do it all the time. They swoop in, hit it, and go, but as soon as we do that, they label us! Now my life is ruined. I've been a dancer all my life and want to go to college for dance, but they want to kick me off of the team because of this.

You don't understand how this feels. They wrote in paint on my brand-new car! This is horrible!"

Consoling a frantic Willow, Sanaa uttered, "We'll get it off."

"You'd help me?" Willow stopped freaking out and asked, stunned that this practical stranger cared.

"Yes, I'd help you because I can't tell you how you feel, but I know how horrible this list is making me feel. We're going to beat this. You with me?"

Willow nodded. Sanaa smiled. Both of the girls were happy that, through the madness, they now knew they weren't alone.

***

All day in school, Willow and Sanaa texted each other. One exchange touched them both.

"Just thinking of ya and had to say . . . keep ur head up," Sanaa wrote.

Willow texted back, "Good now. Ur right, they won't beat us."

The girls sat with each other during lunch and agreed to meet after school. Sanaa knew a shop where a guy was reasonable and could fix practically anything. As soon as the last bell rang, they met up near the gym. Willow wanted to let the dance instructor, Ms. Seely, know that she couldn't stay for practice, but the two continued to connect as they gave each other compliments.

"You know why you got a bunch of haters?" Sanaa asked.

"No, why?" Willow asked.

"Because they wish they had a body like yours."

"If I had your cute face, I certainly wouldn't be worrying about none of these chumps," Willow told Sanaa.

They both giggled, confident that they were cuter and finer than any haters they had at Jackson High School. The laughter was good for them. As glares turned their way, they didn't sweat the drama.

After they were in the hallway alone, Willow took a shortcut down the vo-tech hallway. No one used these classrooms, so the hall was dark and empty. Usually.

Sanaa briskly followed until she saw her boyfriend and her best friend locked in an embrace. She was at a loss for words, seeing Miles and Toni all hugged up. Willow was lost at first, but after seeing Sanaa's whole demeanor change, she knew that was Sanaa's boo.

Sanaa turned so quick she ran into a locker, making a loud noise. The sound alerted the two culprits. All they saw was Sanaa's heels as she sprinted back down the hall.

Willow followed. "What is going on? Wait!"

"Just . . . leave me alone."

"What do you mean, leave you alone? You about to help me go and get my car fixed! I'm not leaving! You helped me when I was boo-hooing, now you're doing the same. That's not how I roll. I don't know who's been your friend before, but I'ma be a better one than that. Who needs a beat down? So that guy was your boo?"

"Yes . . ."

"We're going to get this straight right now."

"I can't confront him!"

"Why not?"

"Because that was my best friend! She's

always liked him. He and I connected, and I . . ."

"What? You got with the guy she liked? You can't help it if he liked you."

"She would never see it like that."

Before they could get outside, Miles caught up and grabbed her. "Sanaa, I need to explain. It's not what you thought you saw."

"Get your hands off!" Sanaa screamed.

When he didn't let go, Willow got right in his face. "Are you deaf?"

He threw his hands up and walked back in the direction from which he came. Sanaa cried harder, and she fell on Willow's shoulder. Her love affair was over.

"Let it out, girl. I understand. His tail betrayed you, but whatever."

"How could they both do me like this? But if she didn't know he was my guy, then how could I be mad at her?"

"Women know . . . I could see in her eyes she was satisfied you saw what you saw. But you know what? This little thing we have going on, we need to find those other three girls on the list. All of us need to have a meeting because there're some folks around here who are trifling, but they're not going to be able to pull us down if we're united. The authors of this list probably got more dirt than all of us combined."

"I don't want revenge. I just want to be okay," Sanaa said.

"I hear you. Straight up tho', if we stick together maybe we can be strong and united, and stop being rattled."

CHAPTER TWELVE
Fixed (Willow's Ending)

When Willow pulled into her driveway, she was relieved on so many fronts. One, her parents were not home. Two, the paint was successfully cleaned from her hood. And three, she was actually very happy that she and Sanaa were developing a friendship.

Before getting out of the car, she smiled, thinking of how much she really admired Sanaa. It's not like she really knew her, but she remembered seeing her around school. Not only was Sanaa flawless on the outside, truly a model-type, but she also always seemed happy—at least before the swoop list. Willow wanted some of that to rub off on her, and maybe, with their newfound friendship, it could. As soon as Willow got out of the car, she was astonished to see her next-door neighbor, Dawson, standing there.

"We need to talk," Dawson said.

"I'm trying to get in my house."

"Fine."

Dawson stepped out of the way, opened up the backseat car door, and grabbed her book bag. This wasn't abnormal. From time to time, when she was struggling with too much stuff, he'd always be there, like a knight in shining armor, to help get her inside. She was always impressed that Dawson was super smart. Now she noticed he had developed some nice muscles recently—and lost his braces.

Willow liked to tease him, but deep down she thought he was a good guy and appreciated his help.

"I don't need any help with anything today," she said when she got to her front door.

Ignoring her, Dawson grabbed the keys, unlocked the door, and followed her inside.

He had an open-door policy to be at her house while her parents were away. They used to be tighter than glue when they were little, but they'd grown apart when Willow gravitated to the party scene and Dawson took the scholar track.

"What do you want, Dawson? I don't have no snacks in here. My mom didn't leave nothing for you. Go home," Willow said, remembering from long ago when Dawson would come over after school and pig out.

"We need to talk about this list," Dawson said, holding up his phone and displaying a photo of the list.

"You're just now finding out about that? You're late. Need to get your head out of a book, boy," Willow said, trying to blow it off.

"I'm serious, Willow. Guys are talking about you giving it up freely and . . ."

"And what? You gonna try and fix me? Or is this what you want?" Willow laid a big kiss on his cheek.

He pulled away. "You know that's not what I want."

"You know what I'm about. Get out." She opened up the door, pushed him out, and closed it.

Dawson stood on the outside, a hand on his cheek. She stood on the inside of the door, wondering why she was so cruel to the one she knew actually cared about her.

***

Willow was startled when she woke up from her nap. Dawson was standing over her. For a minute Willow didn't know whether she was awake or dreaming, because all she could think about was pulling Dawson on top of her and getting busy.

She really wanted to beat herself up when Dawson said, "Why you pulling all on your blouse and scrunching around like that? Wake up!"

Fixing her clothes and sitting up, she gave him the true Willow brush-off. "Why you in my bedroom, trying to ask me what I'm doing?"

Grabbing her hand, Dawson said, "We got to go!"

Jerking back, she said, "Go where?"

"Your brother has been in a car accident."

"He doesn't even have his license or a car."

"He wrecked yours!" Dawson told her.

"What!"

Her brother, William, was a true pain in the neck. He was always into mischief. She did have extra keys, but her parents had those. How did her brother take her car? And more importantly, she wondered, was he okay? Dawson sensed her panic and put his hand on her shoulder to assure her.

"Where is he?"

"Not that far from the house. We'll probably be able to get there before the police."

"I can't believe Will did this."

Will had run her car off the road less than three miles away from their home. As they neared the accident scene in Dawson's car, Willow couldn't sit still in the passenger's side. She just kept rocking, wondering why something was always going wrong.

They pulled up to her wrecked car. She wasn't happy to see that the left side of her car had collided with a speed limit sign on the road. Thankfully, Will was okay.

Flashing lights were headed their way. Both Dawson and Willow were nervous, trying to figure out how they would help Will. As much as her little brother got on her nerves, she had his back.

Quickly she said to Dawson, "Just pull over. They won't see me get out. You can say you called me from my brother's phone. I'm going to tell them I was driving."

"What?" Dawson asked as if he was surprised she'd be so honorable.

"Just pull over. I'm not the uncaring witch you think I am. Though I'll probably be grounded from here to eternity because of this."

"Wait. We'll explain to your parents what happened."

"Just pull over, Dawson. I don't need to think about this any more."

"Well maybe you should. This could add points on your record. Plus, you don't want to tell the cops something and then change it around with your parents. Your brother needs to learn a lesson too."

"I thought you wanted me to take up for him," Willow said before she got out of the car.

"Sis," William said, relief in his eyes

"Get in the car with Dawson."

"What do you mean?" William asked.

"You don't have a license. I'll say I was driving."

"For real?"

"You called me down here. And how'd you get my keys, anyway?"

"You said I could take the car."

Stunned, Willow shouted, "I did not!"

"Okay you were sleep, and I don't think you really understood what I was saying, but you didn't say I couldn't take it."

"Urgh, you frustrate me."

Even after Willow explained everything to the cop, she still ended up getting a citation. Thankfully, the car was drivable, and she was able to take it to the guy Sanaa knew. Willow texted her parents from the shop and told them there had been a small car accident. She knew her life would be much easier if she told the truth—that her brother hijacked the car—but they idolized her brother. He was the child who, in their eyes, always did the right thing. For some reason she wanted to protect that, so she confirmed what they already believed, that she was the careless one.

That night when her parents were screaming at her, Will and Dawson were trying to take up for her, but her folks weren't trying to hear their words. Her brother could have made sure they knew the truth, but he was scared. She knew how to handle the scrutiny. When they walked away, she and Dawson were alone.

He gently took her hand, smiled her way, and said, "I'm proud of you."

"For what?" she questioned. "I lie down, and I'm a doormat."

"Yeah, but this time it's not for a selfish cause, which makes me believe there is hope for you," Dawson said as he stroked her cheek.

"Whatever, I'm so broken there's no way I can be fixed."

CHAPTER THIRTEEN
Tried (Olive's Ending)

All weekend long Olive did her best to put the whole swoop list thing out of her mind. When she was at the group home, nobody mentioned it. They weren't the most scholarly bunch, but something must have shaken them all up, because for most of the weekend they were locked away, studying. Olive knew she was going to have to buckle down, and she wanted Shawn and Charles to do the same. The three of them were the seniors in the house. Because of their situation, they could get financial aid for college, but first they had to qualify to get into a school. Getting better test scores was the first step.

As she walked into school on Monday, she had it all set in her mind to come ready to be a sponge and soak in everything her instructors were teaching. But she was rattled right off the bat when she got a text from Tiger that read, "Charles and Shawn are dead. I might rethink it if you give my boys a treat again. You have 'til the end of the day. Be at the car, or be at the morgue."

She rushed into the school bathroom and started shaking. She didn't even realize she wasn't alone. Then she saw she was being watched and looked over in the corner to see exactly who it was. Olive spotted the fast girl, Willow. She didn't know her personally, but she knew of her. Willow ran with the popular crowd. Being a dancer, Willow was everything Olive wished she could be, except for the bad reputation. Now she realized the two of them were hooked together thanks to the swoop list. She'd run into Willow several times before, but Willow never had the time for her. Now Olive caught the popular chick's attention.

"You're Olive, right?" Willow asked.

Olive nodded. "Yeah."

"Sanaa, come on out," Willow said as she tapped on the stall.

"Give me a second, dang," a voice shouted back.

"It's another swoop list girl," Willow explained to Olive.

Suddenly they heard the toilet flush. Swoop list girl number one came flying out the stalls. She washed her hands, squinted at Willow for rushing her, and then looked at Olive.

"I'm Sanaa. You okay?"

Olive shook her head. She looked away. Both Willow and Sanaa felt her pain.

"We get it," Willow said. "People think I'm all tough and can take it, but we know being on this list is cruel."

"I can't believe my ex took advantage of me," Olive said, shocked she was opening up. It was so effortless to reveal her inner thoughts. Did the three of them have a connection because of this list? Was it as healthy as it seemed to her? She didn't have answers, but all she knew was at first she was shaking, but now she felt strong.

She didn't have answers, but it appeared she had comrades. Olive breathed, thankful she had people who understood. Could there be a friendship growing?

***

Ten minutes after the bell rang, signaling the end of the day, Olive met up with Sanaa and Willow, and they were keeping it real. She was so thankful she didn't have to stand alone to face Tiger. It was one thing to bully a girl all alone, but it was another thing to mess with a girl who had backup.

Olive said, "I'm glad I can talk to you guys. Being from the group home, I've never had any girlfriends, but . . ."

Sanaa put her hand on Olive's shoulder and said, "Doesn't matter our background; we're all in this together. This school thinks they're going to take us down."

"Yep, I have a bunch of so-called friends who are happy we're going through this," Willow piped up.

"That's wrong," Olive said. "But we'll show them."

All three girls giggled. That was until Olive started shaking again when she saw Tiger walking her way. Willow stepped in front of her.

Willow rolled her eyes at Tiger and said, "Keep it moving, Olive! Forget him."

Tiger stepped to her and undressed her with his eyes. "Willow, I knew it was only a matter of time before the two of y'all connected."

Willow said, "Move."

Tiger leaned around Willow, looked straight at Olive, and said, "Maybe you can pick up a couple pointers from this one. I heard she knows how to give good . . ."

"Whatever!" Willow yelled as she pushed Tiger.

"Let's go, girls," Sanaa said, putting her arm around Olive and making her turn her back to Tiger. "I'm so glad you're done with him."

"Yeah, but he ain't done with me," Olive said as she looked at her cell to reread the text message. Olive started shaking again. Willow and Sanaa read the text. They both knew this was serious.

***

When Olive saw Tiger go to the policeman in the school parking lot, she knew Tiger was up to something. If she didn't figure it out, it was going to be big trouble for her foster brothers. Her eyes scoured the parking lot to find them.

"Oh my gosh!" Olive said. "The cops are going over there to Charles and Shawn."

"Those are your foster brothers?" Sanaa asked.

Olive nodded. "We got to get over there. I know Tiger told some lie on them."

So the three of them bolted across the parking lot, and sure enough the cop was grilling them. The tall officer said, "Well, in the incident that happened at school last week, I heard one of you had the gun."

"Who told you that?" said Charles, standing to his full height, an inch above the cop.

"Just want to let y'all know, I'll be watching you. Pulled up your rap sheets, and you two got juvenile offenses a mile long," the officer threatened.

"Arrest us," Charles dared.

"You better watch your tone, boy," the cop said as he got closer to Charles.

Olive couldn't help herself, and she pulled Charles back. He was about to go off until he saw it was her. Their eyes connected. She really did care about him. Willow and Sanaa talked to the officers. Shawn was distracted by some girl who called him away.

Charles said, "I'm not going to let him punk me. I don't even care if he is a policemen."

"But he wasn't lying about your record. You can't get any more trouble. We're this close to getting out of here. Don't screw it up, especially not for me. I don't need you getting involved."

"I'm already involved. They mess with you, they mess with me," he said.

Chills went up and down her spine. She couldn't help it. She was feelin' Charles in a deeper way. He wasn't just a foster brother anymore. Something else was going on, and she couldn't fight that strong feeling, no matter how hard she tried.

CHAPTER FOURTEEN

Needed (Octavia's Ending)

Octavia was smiling from ear to ear as she stood in front of Shawn. Moments earlier he was all frazzled, with the police in his face, but now he was standing before her, and he was relaxed. Octavia was turning pink, eating up the connection as if it was a meal.

"You know I want to get to know you more," Shawn said to her.

Octavia batted her eyes. "I'd like that."

Things got intense when one of the girls, Olive, rushed over and stood between her and Shawn. "Back up, chick! What you doing all in my brother's face?"

"Your brother?" Octavia asked, trying not to appear punkish.

Olive stepped to her real strong. "You heard me. He's my white brother. He don't need no lying trailer trash girl trying to bring him down."

"Wait a minute, Olive," Shawn piped in. "I can talk for myself."

"You stay out of this," Olive turned to Shawn and scolded. "Charles, you better get him."

Charles came over and said, "Man, come on."

Shawn was upset Olive was getting on his friend. He tried to intervene, but Charles stood in the way. Olive got even closer to Octavia, silently giving her the message to leave.

"What do you have against me? What do you want to say to me?" Octavia demanded.

"You ain't never want to be with Shawn before. I remember you the other day at the fight."

"I was pulling him away from it."

"Not how I remember it. You wanted him to go with you, and the cops were coming in that same direction. Thankfully, he went with us, but now the cops are questioning him again, and you're all around. What you want to do? Get him to hit it, and you holler rape or something?"

"That's enough, Olive," Shawn cut in and said.

Octavia was getting teary-eyed as a crowd was gathering. She didn't want there to be issues, so she threw her hands up. Turning, she ran straight into Ms. Davis. Octavia apologized and then tried to flee.

Ms. Davis held her shirt. "Nope, you stay. Olive, Sanaa, and Willow . . . I want to see all of you guys in my office first thing tomorrow. We are going to deal with this swoop list thing once and for all. Tensions are getting a little too hot around here."

"Ms. Davis, with all due respect, I done already talked to you," Willow said.

"I don't need no meeting with her," Olive uttered, shocked and a bit annoyed that Octavia was even on the list.

"Well, you gonna have one. Tomorrow morning," Ms. Davis insisted.

All the girls looked at each other. Although frustrated, they knew they didn't have a choice.

Octavia felt real uneasy that the other three weren't digging her. She tried to tell herself she didn't care, but deep down she did.

***

Octavia was the first to arrive at Ms. Davis's office. Her goal was to catch her before anyone else came in. She had much to share. Ms. Davis was so in tune to what was going on that she could look at Octavia and tell she was intimidated.

"Relax," Ms. Davis said.

Octavia vented, "These girls don't like me. It's my senior year of high school. I've been a loner for a reason. You'd think I was a goth girl or something the way people stay away from me. I smile at a guy, and a girl who's not even his blood wants to check me. It's just not right."

"You and I have always kept it real, Octavia," Ms. Davis said. "I know it's tough for you being a minority at this school. However, just because they're not blood, as you call it, doesn't mean Olive doesn't see her foster brother as someone she's got deep ties to. Honestly, I've got some family I won't claim. They stab you in the back the first chance they get. They don't want you to be nothing or have nothing. And they're always looking for a handout but never try to help. Your home life might not be perfect either. Nobody's at this school is. Most of the kids from great families that got it going on around these parts, let's face it, they're in a private school. Most of you guys who are here are here because you have to be here."

"Why are you saying this to me, Ms. Davis? What's the big deal?"

"I'm saying, as bad as you might think your life is, imagine having no parents. Cut Olive slack. Her life is tough."

"Well, she needs to get off my back."

"Maybe what she needs is a friend."

"She's got that in those other swoop girls."

"Honey, you're one of them."

As Olive, Sanaa, and Willow entered Ms. Davis's office together, Octavia sat back and pondered Ms. Davis's words, realizing she had a point. Maybe this session was going to be crucial to help give her perspective and to help get her to a better place. However, when Olive looked her way and rolled her eyes, Octavia wasn't sure.

"Oh, you're in here already," Olive said, sneering at Octavia.

"Okay, we're not going to have any of that," Ms. Davis said. "Olive, sit down, girl."

"Yeah, quit acting all tough," Willow said to her. "Don't make me get Tiger."

Octavia inwardly smiled. She was thinking all three girls were against her, but when she saw Sanaa nudge Olive to make her chill out, and after hearing Willow's comment, she realized she didn't have a problem with all three girls, just one—which was still bad, but it could have been worse.

"Where is Pia?" Ms. Davis asked. "I saw her in the hallway yesterday after I talked to you four and invited her as well."

"I got a test next period," Olive said. "Can we just start this? I don't see this whole bonding thing working out anyway. We connect with whom we connect with."

"Oh, don't even trip," Willow told her. "You ain't seem to mind us having your back. Maybe if you get to know Octavia, you can cut her some slack."

Sanaa nodded. Ms. Davis nodded as well. In walked Pia. Of all the girls, Octavia admired this Hispanic beauty the most. After all, she was a cheerleader with a pretty great reputation—until now.

Ms. Davis began. "Okay, all you guys are here. I want all of our time, though quick, to be meaningful. Let's get to it. Kids at this school have been cruel, and in talking to you individually, I know some part of the swoop list has hurt you."

"A large part," Pia uttered.

"You can say that again," Sanaa echoed.

"Turned my world upside down," Olive confessed.

"Contrary to what the crazy list states, we ain't the worst ones in this school. Just sayin'," Willow shared.

They all looked at Octavia for her to shed light on how she felt, but she didn't feel the same as them. She knew, deep down, the other girls had been done wrong. Deserving or not, someone set out to hurt them. But in truth, Octavia alone had hurt herself.

Trying to be real, she explained, "If I could take back what I did, I would."

"Whatever, being on this list is not your fault," Willow said.

"Yeah, we all got haters, even if we don't know who they are," Olive said. "You don't need to blame yourself."

Octavia looked at Olive with thankful eyes. The group Ms. Davis had formed was gelling. They were all trying to encourage Octavia. She knew she had to say something to give back.

"We can't let this list crush us," Octavia said.

"That's wassup," Willow bellowed as the others smiled.

Ms. Davis appeared pleased. "I am going to work with the principal and your teachers to come up with a time when we will continue to get together. Octavia's right. This list is not going to crush you. You can help each other get stronger and be better. This group is what you all needed."

CHAPTER FIFTEEN
Conquered (Pia's Ending)

For most, the month had blown by. It was the last Friday in January, and many at the school were excited because there was a big home basketball game to be played later that evening. To get folks in the spirit, it was twin day. The idea was to dress up like each other. The swoop list girls had a plan to school their classmates.

Pia didn't have any particular problem with the other girls on the swoop list. Pia was distant, though, as she was dealing with what she'd done. There was no way she could be excited about a growing friendship when she felt like she was a murderer.

While she didn't think being on the swoop list was anything to be proud of, she realized those were the only girls who understood some of what she was going through. She still had her best friend Claire on the cheerleading team, but even she was starting to look at her all crossed-eyed and funny. So when Willow had the idea for the five of them to dress alike on twin day, telling them all they needed to do was give her ten dollars, and she would take care of the rest, Pia agreed. However, Pia's eyes went buck wild when she saw the bright red sweatshirt that displayed the bold words on the front "I'm a proud swoop list girl," and on the back were their names.

"You expect me to wear this?" Pia said to Willow.

"What's the problem, Miss Cheerleader? I'm on the dance team. I know we have uniforms we're supposed to wear for tonight, but ain't nobody thinking about them. I'm sure your girls have been dogging you out just like mine have. So, let's just keep it real. If they realize we ain't taking ourselves too seriously, all of the ugliness will stop. I know you ain't chicken, right?"

"Might as well be," Sanaa said, frowning at the shirt but taking it from Willow.

Olive grinned and said, "Yeah, come on. We got gangs in this school. We've been on the hot seat for two weeks now. Let's cool them off."

"Or show them how hot we really can be," Octavia said, wanting the attention wearing the sweatshirt would bring.

"Look at you!" Olive said, nudging Octavia. "Might be hope for you after all."

Pia, Sanaa, and Willow were pleased to see those two bonding finally. Pia tried on the shirt, and it totally made her feel weird. She wasn't one for big scenes.

"Alright, y'all sure about this?" Pia asked.

"We can do this," Willow assured her.

"Let's go!" Octavia cheered.

The five of them strutted out into the hallway like never before. They got a ton of whistles. As down as Pia had been, she actually was thankful to smile a bit. They walked past a bunch of girls coughing, "Ho."

Willow yelled out, "It takes one to know one! You want a sweatshirt?"

A crowd of boys got behind them like they were rock stars or something. Their bond was real, and this stunt symbolized that they weren't crushed. Pia was happy she participated.

***

"Who dat? Who dat? Who dat think they bad? Who dat? Who dat? We're gonna kick them in their . . ." *Clap, clap, clap* echoed from the Jackson High cheerleaders later that night.

The gym was packed. Everyone seemed excited to be in the building, except Pia. Her mom told her she'd understand if Pia quit the team, and there was certainly a bunch of pressure from her fellow cheerleaders to drop off too. However, Pia knew her mom had done some tricks to come up with the money for the booster fee, and she didn't want those dollars, no matter how triflingly they were acquired, to go to waste. More importantly, Pia had pride. She wasn't as feisty as Willow and Olive, but she wasn't as laid-back as Sanaa and Octavia either. Nobody was going to force her off.

"Cheer hard for us tonight, alright?" came

from Stephen Garcia, the star basketball player tying a shoe near her.

Pia remembered that his voice sounded familiar. Maybe it wasn't an exact match of one of the three guys who had raped her, but something was close to it. If he thought she was up for another round, he had another thing coming. Not only did she carry Mace in her purse now, she also carried a pocketknife.

"Come on, Pia!" Claire shouted, seeing her moving slow.

"Yeah, come on!" Chancy, the cheerleader, yelled out at her.

Pia didn't feel like cheering, and she didn't know how to verbalize that she felt her world was spinning out of control. As she just stood there while they were doing opening cheers, Chancy came and got in her face. Willow, who wasn't dancing, quickly got up from the bleachers and cameto Pia's defense. The two were going at it.

"She should have been kicked off like you!" Chancy screamed out.

"Heifer, you don't know nothing. I wasn't kicked off of dance team. But if you want to see a kick, turn your tail around, and I'll give you a beat down you'll never forget," Willow told her.

"Are you okay?" Willow asked, snapping in Pia's face to wake her from her daze.

"I just need some water," Pia uttered.

Pia hadn't been eating or sleeping. Not taking care of herself was getting the best of her. Striving for something to fight for, she went to Willow and said, "I appreciate you."

Pia then hugged Willow real tight and started crying. The cheerleading coach came over and told Pia to take a break and scolded the girls for fussing. Pia fled to the hall. All the swoop girls followed her out and surrounded her.

"You know, we need a girls' night," Sanaa said.

Willow said, "I'm on restriction. Can we have it at my place? I can probably make that fly."

Olive and Octavia smiled. Sanaa told them she was down. Everyone was in, except Pia.

"Okay, fine," Pia uttered when they wouldn't stop staring.

When she said yes, the other four cheered louder than the cheerleaders on the court. Pia looked at them, and though she'd said yes, she felt bad because she really didn't want to—worse than that, she felt like truly didn't want to live.

***

Pia stood shaking as she looked at herself in the bathroom mirror. She wanted to wipe away the shame. She was at the slumber party with the other swoop list girls, but she wasn't enjoying herself like they were. She opened up her purse, and pulled out bottles of Pamprin and Advil. She was ready to consume all the contents.

With her hands full of pills, she was startled when Willow pounded on the door. "Hey! I got to go."

"One second," Pia said with a desperate cry.

"What's wrong?" Willow asked, hearing the sadness.

"Go away."

"No, this is my house."

As soon as she started to move the pills to her mouth, the four girls burst into the door. They quickly assessed the trouble. Luckily, Pia hadn't swallowed any pills yet. Willow flung the pills from Pia's hand.

"What are you doing?" Willow yelled.

Pia dropped, but Sanaa caught her and said, "We're going to get through this. I've felt horrible this month too, but we have each other now. Don't give up on life."

Pia screamed, "I don't want to be here anymore! You don't understand!"

Olive said, "I understand, try living with no parents. If I can keep going, you can too!"

Pia squealed in desperation, "But at least whoever it was had you. I was pregnant, and I didn't keep my baby, okay? I deserve to be in hell."

The other four girls looked at each other. They knew what they had to do. Not knowing all the circumstances, they weren't going to let their fellow girl stay in her pit of gloom. They loved on her, hugged on her, and encouraged her.

After about two hours, all five of them were in Willow's room, and Pia shared, "I can't thank you all enough. I wanted it to be the end, but after hearing y'all out, I realized this can be a new beginning. Not that I won't carry around this pain, but I'm not going to let those three monsters who raped me beat me mentally."

"None of this was your fault," Sanaa said. "You aren't like me. One thing I learned about from the swoop list was that I was doing everything for this one guy. I didn't respect myself. When I needed him to stand by me, his tail was nowhere around. Probably put me on the list. But he's not getting any anymore. Pia, I don't deserve to be on the list, and you don't deserve to be on the list either."

Willow chimed in. "Yeah, you don't deserve it. I was real promiscuous, but I know I don't deserve this either. Thought what was done in the dark would stay that way. One of those chumps told. I'm on lockdown for now. I want the next guy I'm with to be someone who I actually like. I know I deserve that. They're not having their way with me no more." Willow thought about how she'd taken the fall for her brother's car accident. She knew she had a good heart.

"Well, I'm never going to doing dumb stuff because my boyfriend asked me to again,"

Olive asserted. "I need to be with someone who respects me and doesn't just use me. So we're in unison, Sanaa. I took too many risks, and I'm not doing it anymore. What about you, Octavia?"

Octavia hesitated, then admitted, "I learned that being pure isn't a bad thing. I'm done thinking that it is. I know I'm being cryptic, but I've got to give up being jealous of girls I think have all the fun."

Pia shared, "I wasn't asking to be raped. What happened to me wasn't my fault. None of us deserved to be on that list."

The girls were having a real talk. They made a pact to give up their trifling ways, keep each other accountable, and find out why a dead girl would be sending a letter. Pia wasn't healed, but she was inspired. Sanaa felt that Pia should talk to Ms. Davis about joining a support group for rape victims and going to counselor to help her deal with the fear she still felt every day. Pia hadn't wanted to do it before, but after tonight, she realized that it was helpful to talk about what had happened to her.

Pia smiled for the first time in a long time and said, "Maybe the swoop list has been an eye-opener for all of us. I hate that any of us were on it, but at least we got each other, and at least we now realize the flaws we've conquered."

ACKNOWLEDGMENTS

Give it up . . . need I say more. Whatever you're doing that is keeping you from reaching your full potential . . . let it go! You only have time for things that propel you forward. Here is a big thank you to the people that keep me accountable:

To my parents, thank you for making me give up negative thinking. You helped me to know with hard work, I can reach my dreams. To my publisher, thank you for helping me give up playing it safe. To my extended family, thank you for helping me give up procrastination. You push me to get the books done. To my assistants Shaneen Clay, Alyxandra Pinkston, and Candace Johnson, thank you for helping me give up mediocrity. Your help makes my work top-notch. To my dear friends, too numerous to name, thank you for helping me give up fear. Your friendships make me strong. To my teens, Dustyn, Sydni, and Sheldyn, thank you helping me give up disorganization. Being your mom makes we want things in order. To my husband, thank you for helping me give up stress. Having you as a partner frees my heart. To my readers, especially the kids in Jackson, GA, who gave me the idea for the series, thank you for helping me give up complacency. Your truth about what's really going on in high school helps me get real in the fiction books. And to my Savior, thank you for helping me give up doubt. You always open doors for my writing, clearly showing me I'm fulfilling my purpose. Thank you, Lord.

ABOUT THE AUTHOR

STEPHANIE PERRY MOORE is the author of more than sixty young adult titles, including the Sharp Sisters series, the Grovehill Giants series, the Lockwood Lions series, the Payton Skky series, the Laurel Shadrach series, the Perry Skky Jr. series, the Yasmin Peace series, the Faith Thomas Novelzine series, the Carmen Browne series, the Morgan Love series, the Alec London series, and the Beta Gamma Pi series. Mrs. Moore is a motivational speaker who enjoys encouraging young people to achieve every attainable dream. She lives in the greater Atlanta area with her husband, Derrick, and their three children. Visit her website at www.stephanieperrymoore.com.

READ ALL THE BOOKS IN THE
SWOOP LIST SERIES:

THE *SWOOP* LIST SANNA
GIVE IT UP

THE *SWOOP* LIST WILLOW
ON YOUR KNEES

THE *SWOOP* LIST OLIVE
BACK THAT THING

THE *SWOOP* LIST OCTAVIA
FEEL REAL GOOD

THE *SWOOP* LIST PIA
SIT ON TOP

THE **SHARP** SISTERS

THE **SHARP** SISTERS

Make Something
of It

STEPHANIE PERRY MOORE

THE **SHARP** SISTERS

Better Than
Picture Perfect

STEPHANIE PERRY MOORE

THE **SHARP** SISTERS

Turn Up
for Real

STEPHANIE PERRY MOORE

THE **SHARP** SISTERS

Truth and
Nothing But

STEPHANIE PERRY MOORE

THE **SHARP** SISTERS

Icing on the Cake

STEPHANIE PERRY MOORE